Babies in Reptarland

KLASKY CSUPO INC.

Based on the TV series *Rugrats*® created by Arlene Klasky, Gabor Csupo, and
Paul Germain as seen on Nickelodeon®

SIMON SPOTLIGHT
An imprint of Simon & Schuster Children's Publishing Division
1230 Avenue of the Americas
New York, New York 10020

Manufactured in the United States of America

First Edition
2 4 6 8 10 9 7 5 3 1

ISBN 0-689-83337-7

Babies in Reptarland

Adapted by Becky Gold
Based on the Script by
David N. Weiss & J. David Stem
and Jill Gorey & Barbara Herndon
and Kate Boutilier

Illustrated by Barry Goldberg

Simon Spotlight/Nickelodeon

New York   London   Toronto   Sydney   Singapore

The babies could hardly believe their luck. Yesterday they were home watching TV and being bossed by Angelica. Today they were in Paris, France, at the Reptarland theme park!

Tommy's daddy had made a giant Reptar robot for Reptarland. The director of the theme park, Coco LaBouche, called to invite everyone to Paris. Stu thought she must be very happy with his invention.

Everyone took the elevator to Coco's office. When they
got there, Kira, Coco's assistant, greeted them.
"Welcome to Reptarland!" she said with a smile.

"Wow," said Angelica as she peeked inside Coco's office. "What's Reptar's head doing in there?" She took a closer look and saw a huge bowl of chocolates on Coco's table. She ran inside, and the babies followed behind her.

Coco was *not* pleased to see them. "Jean-Claude, call the dogcatcher, the exterminator, do something!" she screamed.

"Yes, madame," said Jean-Claude, Coco's helper. "Kira!"

Kira rounded up the babies and sent Stu inside Coco's office. The door slammed shut. "Listen, Pickles," she shouted. "I want that giant tin can *fixed*! And it had better be *perfect* in time for the opening of our Princess Spectacular!"

"That lady sounds really mean, Tommy," Chuckie said.

"She sure does," Tommy agreed.

"Why don't we take the babies to see the Princess Parade?" Kira suggested to Chas.

"That'll be funner," said Phil, as Kira led everyone away from Coco's office.

Later Coco's boss, Mr. Yamaguchi, called her on the phone. He was looking for someone to take his place as head of Reptar Industries. "They must have a family of their own and understand how to bring joy to children," Mr. Yamaguchi said.

"Hmmm," Coco said as she hung up. "How hard can it be to find a man who's already got a brat of his own?"

Suddenly the chocolate bowl fell to the floor. *Crash!*

"Oops!" said Angelica as Coco picked her up by the collar.

Angelica thought fast. "I know a man with a brat," she said. She told Coco all about Chuckie and his daddy. Coco was interested—*very* interested.

"And in return for my help," Angelica finished, "I'd like my own fashion show and my own float in the parade and to be the flower girl at your wedding!"

Coco rolled her eyes.

Meanwhile the Princess Parade was in full swing. The babies listened while Kira told them the story of the princess.

Once upon a time, she began, in a faraway land, there lived a mighty dinosaur named Reptar. The people were afraid Reptar would destroy their village, so they made him live in the forest. There he saw a beautiful princess who was not afraid of him. She didn't think he was scary, she saw he was lonely and unhappy.

"She promised to take care of him forever and ever," Kira finished. "Forever and ever," whispered Chuckie, as the princess's magic dust fell all around him. He wished that the princess could be his new mommy.

That night Coco showed up at dinner. It was time for her to meet Chas.

"I'm sorry to interrupt," Kira said to Coco, "but I need your signatures." She gave Coco some papers to sign. Behind her toddled her little girl.

"That must be Kimi," said Chas. "Would she like to come to the park with me and the kids tomorrow?"

"She'd love to!" Coco cooed. "In fact, I planned to spend the day with her there myself!"

"Do you live in Reptarland?" Tommy asked Kimi.

"No, but I gets to come here all the time," she said.

"Have you met the princess?" asked Chuckie.

"Sure. Lots of times. She lives in that castle up on the bowlcano!" Kimi pointed out the window.

The next day Coco took Chas and the babies on the Ooey-gooey Ride.

Suddenly Kimi took off.

"She's gonna hurt herself!" said Chuckie. Then he watched, amazed, as Tommy, Phil, and Lil followed her.

"C'mon, Chuckie! You can do it!" yelled Kimi.

Chuckie hesitated. "I don't know, guys . . . it looks dangerous!" But he took a deep breath and leaped out of the car.

Kimi led the babies through the park. They ran and ran and ran . . . and finally reached the princess's castle on the volcano.

"I told ya I knowed a shortcup," said Kimi.

"That was the longest shortcup I ever tooked," Phil whispered to Lil.

Just then the clock struck, and the princess came out of her castle. The babies waved at her.

"Isn't she prettyful?" said Lil.

A moment later the princess turned and went back inside.

"What're you waitin' for? Go on in!" Kimi told Chuckie.

But Chuckie was too afraid to knock on the door. The knocker was much too scary! He just wasn't brave enough yet to meet the princess.

The next day Chuckie got another chance.

"Ladies and gentlemen, welcome to the Princess Spectacular!" an announcer called out.

Angelica told Coco that Chuckie wanted the princess to be his mommy. That gave Coco an idea. She sneaked backstage.

The Spectacular began. All the villagers ran away from Reptar.

At last the princess came onstage and sang the Princess Spectacular song in a wobbly voice. Then she tripped over her costume, and she almost forgot to pet Reptar.

The babies didn't notice these mistakes.
And when she sprinkled her magic dust on
the babies, no one was happier than Chuckie.

Coco was delighted. She knew once she was married to Chas, Mr. Yamaguchi would make her head of Reptar Industries.

Chas agreed to marry her. The day of their wedding arrived at last.

Coco had just one last thing to take care of: Angelica and the babies.

"Do you see those sticky fingers? Jam-covered mouths? Guilty little faces?" Coco sneered.

Then she grabbed Chuckie's Wawa. "Jean-Claude, take these little terrors away!" she told her helper. "That one too!" she added, pointing at Angelica.

Jean-Claude took the babies to a cold, dark room.

"I'm sorry, guys," said Chuckie. "If I didn't want a princess mom so bad, we wouldn't be in this terrible place."

"Actually, this is all sorta my fault," Angelica said.

The babies stared at her as she explained how she'd helped Coco get Chas to marry her.

"You guys, I can't let that lady marry my daddy!" Chuckie exclaimed. "We gots to stop that wedding!

"Okay, guys, here's the plan," Chuckie said. "Angelica, you keep Jean-Claude busy while we get inside Reptar."

While Jean-Claude read his newspaper, Angelica tied his shoelaces together so he couldn't move.

Then the babies climbed inside Reptar's head and set off into Reptarland.

As soon as Jean-Claude saw they were gone, he stood up . . . and fell over!

Jean-Claude climbed into Robosnail and caught up with Reptar. "Going somewhere?" he asked.

"Sluggy! Sluggy!" said Dil.

The two monsters battled at the top of the Eiffel Tower. Chuckie, at the controls, made Reptar give Robosnail a big karate kick, knocking him over.

"You did it, Chuckie!" said Tommy.

"We're never gonna get to the church on time!" Angelica exclaimed.

"Oh, yes we will!" said Chuckie.

Just then Tommy spotted Coco's car parked in front of Notre Dame Cathedral. But Chuckie wasn't sure he could make Reptar stop. There were so many buttons on the control panel!

Chuckie pushed a blinking red button. Reptar's head flew off with the babies inside. It soared through the air and landed safely on the cathedral steps.

Inside, Chas and Coco were nearly married. "If anyone objects to this union—" the priest began.

"NOOOOOOOOOOOOO!" Chuckie yelled.

Chuckie's first word saved the day. His daddy did not marry Coco. And Chuckie really did get his wish. Six months later his daddy married Kira.

Now Chuckie had a wonderful new mommy and a little sister, too!